WONDER WOMAN™
TALES OF
PARADISE ISLAND

THE TIARA AND THE TITAN

BY
MICHAEL DAHL

ILLUSTRATED BY
OMAR LOZANO

WONDER WOMAN CREATED BY
WILLIAM MOULTON MARSTON

STONE ARCH BOOKS
a capstone imprint

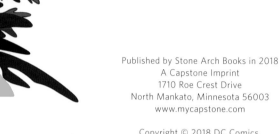

Published by Stone Arch Books in 2018
A Capstone Imprint
1710 Roe Crest Drive
North Mankato, Minnesota 56003
www.mycapstone.com

STAR40368

Library of Congress Cataloging-in-Publication Data is
available on the Library of Congress website.

ISBN: 978-1-5158-3021-4 (library binding)
ISBN: 978-1-5158-3030-6 (paperback)
ISBN: 978-1-5158-3026-9 (eBook PDF)

Summary: A chance encounter on Carnival Island
puts Wonder Woman in pursuit of Giganta and her
greed for gold.

Editor: Christopher Harbo
Designer: Brann Garvey

Printed in the United States of America.
PA021

TABLE OF CONTENTS

BEHOLD, PARADISE ISLAND!

GOLDEN
TIARA

4

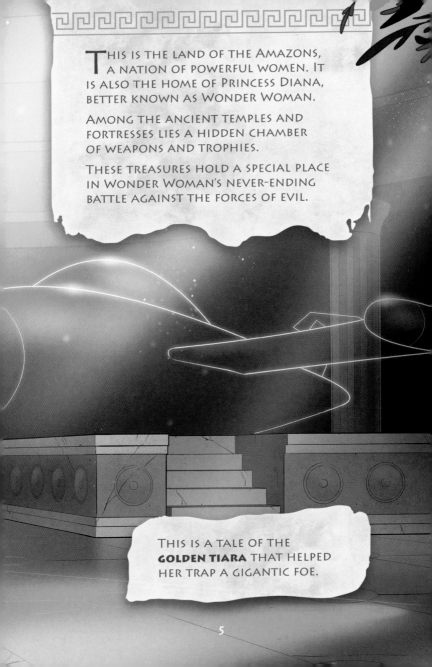

THIS IS THE LAND OF THE AMAZONS, A NATION OF POWERFUL WOMEN. IT IS ALSO THE HOME OF PRINCESS DIANA, BETTER KNOWN AS WONDER WOMAN.

AMONG THE ANCIENT TEMPLES AND FORTRESSES LIES A HIDDEN CHAMBER OF WEAPONS AND TROPHIES.

THESE TREASURES HOLD A SPECIAL PLACE IN WONDER WOMAN'S NEVER-ENDING BATTLE AGAINST THE FORCES OF EVIL.

THIS IS A TALE OF THE **GOLDEN TIARA** THAT HELPED HER TRAP A GIGANTIC FOE.

CHAPTER 1

A HANDFUL OF GOLD

It is midnight in Gateway City Harbor.
The SS *Orion* is docked.

Workers on the docks stare up at the ship.

A huge crane lifts a covered object from the
ship's cargo hold.

The object sways on the crane's cable, high in the air.

RRRRMMMM!

The crane swings toward the docks. It lowers the object to the workers waiting below.

A gentle night breeze lifts the canvas off the mystery object.

One of the workers whistles. "That's solid gold!" he says.

The object is a statue of a beautiful Greek goddess.

"It must be worth millions of dollars!" says another worker.

The dock manager steps toward the statue.

"This is why we had to unload the statue in secret," the manager says. "The police are taking this golden lady to a museum tonight."

AHHHHHHHH!

One of the workers screams and points at the sky. A hand the size of a military tank lowers over the statue.

Then a powerful gust of wind blows across the docks.

FWWWOOOO!

All of the workers fall into the water.

Seconds later, the giant hand and the statue are gone.

CHAPTER 2

CARNIVAL ISLAND

The next day, Wonder Woman and her friend, Steve Trevor, visit Carnival Island.

The island is a giant amusement park. It connects to Gateway City by a long metal bridge.

A puzzled look suddenly crosses Wonder Woman's face.

"Are you still thinking about that statue?" asks Steve.

"The dock workers said they saw a giant hand," says the Amazon. "But that doesn't make sense."

The warm sun shines down. It gleams on Wonder Woman's bracelets and golden tiara.

"You need to take a break from work," says Steve. "Look!"

He points to a colorful sign next to a bright yellow tent.

It reads: THE STRONGEST WOMAN ALIVE!

"Let's check it out," says Steve.

Inside the tent, a large crowd faces a brightly lit stage.

On stage is a man wearing a black coat and hat. He sits on the hood of a dump truck.

The back of the truck is covered by a tarp.

"Ladies and gentlemen," the man says with a sweep of his hand. "I present Herculea, the strongest woman on Earth!"

Into the tent strides a powerful looking woman with red hair. She wears a costume of red and gold.

Wonder Woman grabs Steve's arm.

"That woman!" says the Amazon Princess. "I know her!"

CHAPTER 3

GIGANTA!

The strong woman walks over to the dump truck. She lifts the vehicle and the man above her head.

The crowd gasps. Then they clap.

Wonder Woman steps out from the crowd.

"Giganta!" shouts the Amazon. "You are supposed to be in prison!"

The strong woman sets down the truck and the man.

"No prison can hold me!" Giganta says, pulling the tarp off the truck. "Not when I'm after gold!"

Wonder Woman sees the statue and other gold treasures in the back of the dump truck.

The crowd screams as Giganta grows before their eyes.

As everyone flees the tent, Wonder Woman flings her gold tiara.

SHWIP! SHWIP! SHWIP!

The tiara slices through the tent's ropes. The tent starts to sag. The heavy canvas falls onto Giganta and traps her.

The giant laughs. She keeps growing, and her head rips through the top of the tent.

"I said no one can stop me," yells Giganta.

The Amazon Princess flies up to Giganta's shoulders. "Surrender," says Wonder Woman. "And return the statue."

"You're full of hot air," says Giganta. "And here's some more!"

The titan blows a stream of air at the Amazon. The powerful wind flings the hero far across the carnival.

Wonder Woman lands on the very top of the Ferris wheel.

CHAPTER 4

THE TERRIBLE TITAN

Wonder Woman watches the giant wade toward the bridge in Gateway City Harbor.

Giganta holds the dump truck under her arm.

The giant tugs at one of the bridge's metal beams. "This will keep you busy, Wonder Woman!" says the villain.

The metal beam falls toward a blue car on the bridge.

"Wonder Woman!" yells Steve Trevor from the car. He has been following Giganta's escape.

ZOOOOOOOOM!

Wonder Woman flies like a comet! She reaches the bridge in time to catch the heavy metal beam.

But how can I stop Giganta? she wonders.

Sunlight gleams off the gold treasures inside Giganta's truck. Suddenly, the mighty Amazon has an idea.

CHAPTER 5

TIARA TRAP

"It doesn't matter how big you are," Wonder Woman calls out. "Thank Athena, my gold tiara doubles my brainpower and my strength!"

Giganta stares at the golden tiara and grins. The titan swats at her flying foe with a massive hand.

Wonder Woman's tiara is knocked off her head and lands on the bridge. The Amazon tumbles down into the cold water.

SPLASSSSSSHH!

Giganta reaches for the golden crown.
It looks small in her huge fingers.

ZWWWOOOOZZZZH!

Giganta shrinks down to her normal size.

"This treasure is too great to throw in the
back of my truck!" the villain says.

Giganta places the tiara on her head.

Another gold object flies through the air.

ZING!!

It is Wonder Woman's legendary lasso.
The golden rope wraps around Giganta,
holding her tight.

"I knew you couldn't resist the tiara," says
Wonder Woman. "I also knew you'd have to
shrink down in order to wear it."

Wonder Woman soars into the air, pulling Giganta behind her.

"I'll be back later to repair the bridge," the hero calls out to the people below.

Steve Trevor smiles and waves.

Wonder Woman's not only the strongest woman alive, he thinks. *She's the smartest!*

GLOSSARY

canvas (KAN-vuhs)—a strong, heavy cloth

cargo hold (KAHR-goh HOLD)—the area in a vehicle where objects are stored and carried

comet (KOM-uht)—a fast-moving ball of rock and ice that circles the Sun

foe (FOH)—an enemy

goddess (GOD-iss)—a female god

harbor (HAR-bur)—a place where ships load and unload passengers and cargo

manager (MAN-uh-jur)—a person in charge of a group

tarp (TARP)—a heavy waterproof covering

tiara (tee-AR-uh)—a piece of jewelry that looks like a small crown

titan (TYE-tuhn)—a powerful giant

treasure (TREZH-ur)—gold, jewels, money, statues, or other valuable items that have been hidden

DISCUSS

1. Steve tells Wonder Woman that she should take a break from work. Is he right? Should super heroes take time off? Why or why not?

2. Why does Giganta keep her treasure in a dump truck? What are some advantages to using this type of vehicle?

3. Wonder Woman tricks Giganta into shrinking down in order to capture her. Discuss how the Amazon warrior could have defeated her foe in other ways.

WRITE

1. Giganta has the power to grow larger. Imagine you had the same power. What would you do and where would you go? Write a story about your adventures.

2. Wonder Woman uses her tiara to slice through the ropes of the carnival tent. Imagine if you had a powerful piece of jewelry or clothing. Write a short paragraph describing what it could do.

3. At the end of the story, Wonder Woman flies away with Giganta bound in her lasso. What happens next? Write another chapter that continues the story.

AUTHOR

Michael Dahl is the prolific author of more than 200 books for children and young adults, including *Bedtime for Batman, Be A Star, Wonder Woman!,* and *Sweet Dreams, Supergirl.* He has won the AEP Distinguished Achievement Award three times for his nonfiction, a Teachers' Choice Award from *Learning* magazine, and a Seal of Excellence from the Creative Child Awards. He is also the author of the Batman Tales of the Batcave and Superman Tales of the Fortress of Solitude series. Dahl currently lives in Minneapolis, Minnesota.

ILLUSTRATOR

Omar Lozano lives in Monterrey, Mexico. He has always been crazy for illustration and is constantly on the lookout for awesome things to draw. In his free time, he watches lots of movies, reads fantasy and sci-fi books, and draws! Omar has worked for Marvel, DC, IDW, Capstone, and several other publishing companies.